HOW TO BE A ROCK STAR

written by **LISA TOLIN**

illustrated by **DANIEL DUNCAN**

putnam

G. P. Putnam's Sons

For Smolder, Rock Rebel
and the Tour Manager,
my family band —L.T.

For Jules —D.D.

G. P. Putnam's Sons

An imprint of Penguin Random House LLC, New York

First published in the United States of America by G. P. Putnam's Sons, an imprint of Penguin Random House LLC, 2022

Text copyright © 2022 by Lisa Tolin | Illustrations copyright © 2022 by Daniel Duncan

Library of Congress Cataloging-in-Publication Data | Names: Tolin, Lisa, author. | Duncan, Daniel, illustrator. | Title: How to be a rock star / written by Lisa Tolin; illustrated by Daniel Duncan. | Description: New York: G. P. Putnam's Sons, 2022. | Summary: A child offers advice on starting a rock band, going on tour, and leaving the audience wanting more. | Identifiers: LCCN 2021026495 (print) | LCCN 2021026496 (ebook) | ISBN 9781984814203 (hardcover) | ISBN 9781984814227 (kindle edition) | ISBN 9781984814210 (epub) | Subjects: CYAC: Rock music—Fiction. | Bands (Music)—Fiction. | Family life—Fiction. | LCGFT: Picture books. | Classification: LCC PZ7.1.T6235 Ho 2022 (print) | LCC PZ7.1.T6235 (ebook) | DDC [E]—dc23 | LC record available at https://lccn.loc.gov/2021026495 | LC ebook record available at https://lccn.loc.gov/2021026496

Manufactured in China | ISBN 9781984814203 | 10 9 8 7 6 5 4 3 2 1
TOPL

Design by Eileen Savage | Text set in Cantoria MT Pro | The art was created digitally.

The publisher does not have any control over and does not assume any responsibility for author or third-party websites or their content.

If you want to be a rock star . . .

First, you need a band.

Younger brothers are not ideal, but yours
will have to do.

Here's a little-known fact: Stuffed animals
make excellent backup singers.

Now you need instruments.
Your mom will say,

An electric guitar is too noisy, and a bass is too big, and don't even *think* about a drum kit.

You'll say,

Rock 'n' roll, Mom!

But Mom will not be convinced.

So you'll have to wing it. Grab a broom for a guitar

and some pots and pans for drums.

Find a microphone—or a toilet paper roll—you can shout into. Shouting is important if you're going to be a rock star.

Your band needs a name.
Mom will say,

Dad will say,

Your brother will shout,

You will banish them from rock 'n' roll band naming.
Choose something awesome, but not

—that's mine.

Start off by playing songs everybody knows.

THE WHEELS ON THE BUS...

Sing the whole thing extra-loud to see
how that sounds.

Next, try heavy metal.

Or punk.

Or create a new kind of music,
like heavy-punk-metal-pop.

Your little brother will try to grab your instrument, and your dad will say, "Can you please let your brother have the broom?"

So you'll play tambourine. Nobody said a musician's life would be easy.

Take this time to show
off your dance moves:
Rock 'n' roll jumping.

Moonwalking.

Sliding across the stage on your knees.

After a while, your brother will rip off his tutu.

Mom will ask,

Is that my good scarf?

And Dad will say,

I liked it better when you played "The Wheels on the Bus."

Everyone's a critic.

So take your band on the road.

Play your bedroom.

The bathtub.

The backyard.

By now, you'll be mobbed
by screaming fans.

Your brother might smash your guitar
or have a wardrobe malfunction.

Whatever happens, keep playing.
That's rock 'n' roll.

The tour may take its toll on your brother.

He'll be running in circles with a smear of milk over his mouth.

He may grab your favorite backup singer and run off to another room. It's clear that you have creative differences.

So you'll go solo.
Write a sad song about your brother and the missing backup singer.
You'll think about hanging up your broom . . .

But just like that, your brother and
the backup singer will come back!

Get the band
back together for
a reunion concert.

Play "The Wheels on the Bus,"
for old times' sake.

ENCORE!

the audience will shout.
Look surprised. Play
one more song.

ENCORE!

they'll shout again.

This time, shake your head and bow.
Here's an important rule for rock stars:
Always leave your audience wanting more.